A Fishy Tail

From Siobhan's
Magic Garden Book
3

Written by Nicole Round
and
Illustrated by Tommy Round

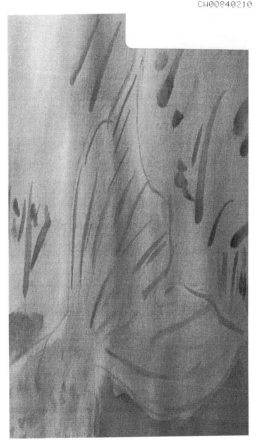

To Max and Madge Harvey
to read together
with love
XXX

Brookes, the fancy
goldfish,
Was mischievous and
vain
And frankly, the folks in
the garden
Thought he could be a
pain.

"Hey Landfish," he would
call,
As you went walking by,
Then squirt water
quickly,
Straight into your eye.

But one evening there
Was a **SPLASH**
And something nearly
Landed on him, **CRASH**.

"What was that?"
Asked Brookes in
fright,
But nothing answered
In the dark, dark night.

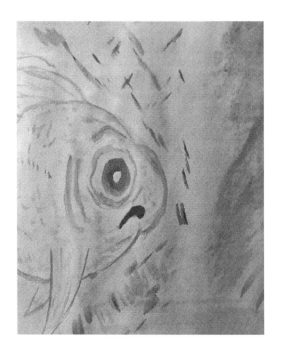

He peered hard
Into that deep dark,
Maybe it was a frog,
A log, a big fish or even
a shark!

Brookes thought as
Hard as a little fish
could,
Then he swam bravely
down
To investigate the
sticky mud.

Down he went, taking
big breaths,
"What if?" said
Brookes, quite pale
"What if, it's a nasty
crocodile
Or a huge gigantic
whale?

What if it is hungry?
And what if, its dream
dish,
Is a great big mouthful
Of handsome fish?"

"Agh!" So up, up, and
away, he swam
To the pools farthest
side,
where he had a secret
place,
a cave in which to hide.

Next day, Brookes
woke up hungry
And went to his food
store
And, being a normal
goldfish,
He had forgotten the
night before.

So happily, he decided
To go out for a swim.
When he heard
Alexander Beetle
Loudly shouting for
him.

"Hello, Alexander
Beetle,
Do you want to play?"
"No, I am sorry
Brookes,
We have an emergency
today."

"Mushroom and Small
are helping,
Searching all around.
Paddles has gone
missing
And he must be found.

This is Puddles, the
wellie boot,
Paddles, is his brother
And wellington boots
are no good,
If they are without the
other."

"That is right,
Alexander Beetle,
Paddles, is as lost as
can be."
"What does he look
like?" asked Brookes.
Puddles said, "Well,
exactly like me."

"I have never seen
you,"
answered Brookes,
"And what is more,"
I have never seen any
Landfish,
That looks quite like
you before."

"Sorry guys, it's
breakfast time.
Nearly my best meal of
the day,
And as I really cannot
help you,
I think I'll be on my
way."

About two minutes
later, he stopped
And Brookes, his
stomach sinking,
Saw through the deep
water,
That a huge eye was
blinking!

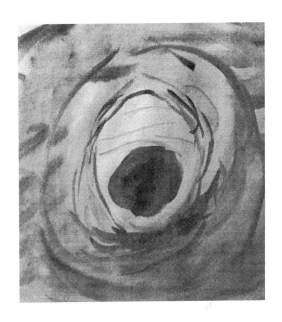

"Monster!" screamed
Brookes,
"I remember now, I
see.
There is a Monster
In my pond, looking up
at me!"

"What is the matter,
Brookes?"
Cried Alexander and
Puddles, unsure.
Brookes stopped and
looked at Puddles.
"I have seen *you*
before."

"Yes, just a few
minutes ago,
Brookes, you look all
pale."
"Wait a minute, I'll be
back
Said Brookes, turning
tail.

So, the brave little fish
returned
Once more, to look.
"Landfish," He
screamed out.
Alexander and Puddles
ducked.

"No, there is a Landfish in my pond.
Please help me, get it out
A Landfish needs air.
It is in trouble; I have no doubt."

"It has got to be Paddles," said Puddles,
"This is as bad as can be.
We are waterproof and rubber,
But we have got to get him free."

"I have a rope," called
Stag the Small,
Arriving just in time.
"Here Brookes, catch"
called Alexander,
Throwing him, a line.

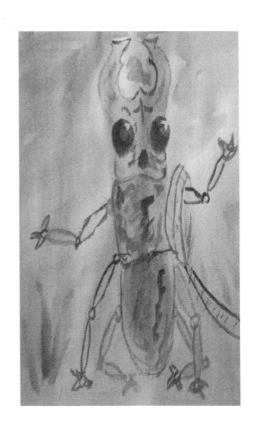

Brookes, wrapped the
rope around Paddles
And the four, pulled
hard up top,
And Paddles went up
to the surface,
Like a cork from a
bottle, **POP**.

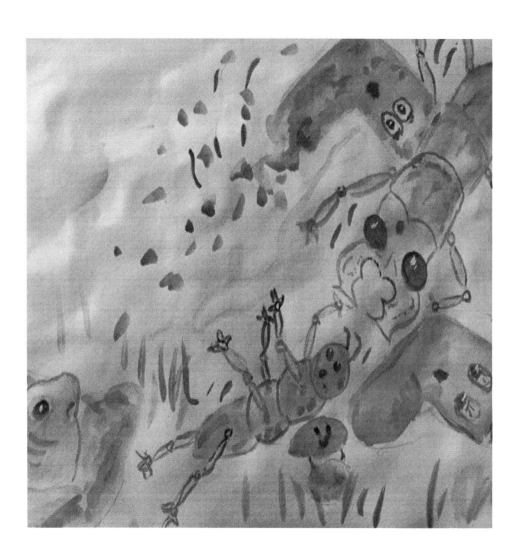

"Thanks everyone,"
said Paddles.
He was such a muddy
sight.
"It was silly playing
near water,
I was stuck so very
tight."

"Landfish, should not
play in water
Unless they can swim,"
Lectured Brookes,
sternly.
While the others
applauded him.

So, Brookes was a hero
And tales of him were
told.
Little ones, heard of,
Brookes,
The handsome. Brookes,
the brave and bold.

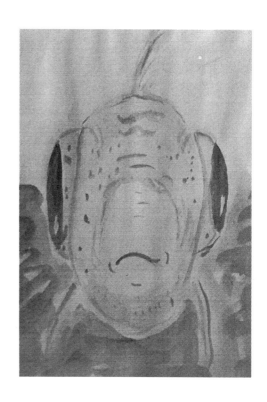

But sometimes Brookes
could not help it,
And as he swam laughing
by,
If he turned and saw a
Landfish,
He would squirt it, in the
eye.

The End

Authors Note:

Brookes is a goldfish and he lives with his friends, Mithras and Small.

They live in a cosy fish tank in my house. One day, when he is big enough, and if he asks nicely, he might live in the pond in the Siobhan's Magic Garden.

Brookes would like everyone to know, he is far too polite to squirt anyone in the eye!

xxxxx

Brookes

the

Goldfish

Wellington Boots

Pond

(Brookes is right. Landfish, should **always** be <u>very</u> careful around water!)

Thanks to:

Siobhan Ramsey - because.

All at Plenty at the Square
in Thornton. The best café in
Bradford bar none and
OPEN once more - hooray.
See them on Facebook and
drool...

All at Sinclairs in Otley,
especially those who have
been forced to read the books,
Caroline, Wendi, Paul, Julia,
Gary, and Jean. There could
be more...

Laronda Kitchen – for
buying all of them!

Tommy, only uses
Art Gecko.
Quality sketchbooks.
Made in Otley.

www.artgeckosketch.com

available on Amazon

Goodbye. Goodbye. Come back to the Magic Garden soon.

We hope you
liked
the story
Love from
Nikki
And
Tommy
XXX

There is a one-off picture
of Mushroom as part of
Tracy Hardaker's
"Thankyou NHS"
rainbow display, on the
windows of the
Sinclairs Factory,
Courthouse Road, Otley.
Well worth a look if you
are in Otley or on social
media, just look up
"Sinclairs Stationery."
She worked very hard
on it, with input from
local children (and
Tommy!)

Coming
Soon:

A Stag-
Beetle's Tale

An Ant's
Tale

Other titles
By Nicole Round

- Seed – A story of a seed and its destiny

By Nicole and Tommy Round

- A Beetle's Tale, from Siobhan's Magic Garden.
- A Millipede's Tale – from Siobhan's Magic Garden Book 2
- A Fishy Tail – from Siobhan's Magic Garden Book 3

Poetry by Nicole Round – adult themes

- Heartburn on a Sea of Minor Obsessions.
- Soulways.
- Learning Ground.

On Amazon available as books or on Kindle.

Coming soon:

- A Stag Beetle's Tale – from Siobhan's Magic Garden Book 4
- An Ant's Tale – from Siobhan's Magic Garden Book 5
- A Fairy Tale

By Nicole Round and Bill Johnston

- The Hotte Dogge Quest

No longer available
By Nicole and Tommy Round

- The Little Embryo

Printed in Poland
by Amazon Fulfillment
Poland Sp. z o.o., Wrocław